HOW TO WRITE A BESTSELLING ACTION & ADVENTURE ROMANCE

NAVY SEALS, FRONTLINE RESPONDERS & OTHER HOT HEROES IN LOVE

JUST BAE

CONTENTS

INTRODUCTION

In the landscape of literary genres, Action & Adventure Romance stands as a testament to humanity's dual desire for both heart-racing excitement and soul-stirring love. This powerful combination has given birth to countless best-sellers and blockbuster films that continue to captivate audiences worldwide. As you embark on your journey to craft your own story in this genre, you'll discover the delicate balance required to weave together pulse-pounding action sequences with tender moments of romantic development. The success of works like "Romancing the Stone" (1984) demonstrates how a romance writer can be thrust into an adventure, creating organic opportunities for both character growth and romantic tension. Understanding the fundamental elements that make this genre unique will be crucial to your success as a writer. The intricate dance between danger and desire creates a narrative framework that keeps readers on the edge of their seats while simultaneously investing in the emotional journey of your characters.

In examining successful examples of the genre, we can look to Diana Gabaldon's "Outlander" series, which masterfully combines historical adventure with a passionate love story that transcends time. The relationship between Claire Randall and Jamie Fraser develops against a backdrop of political intrigue, warfare, and survival in 18th-century Scotland. This series exemplifies how physical dangers can serve as catalysts for emotional intimacy between characters. The external conflicts force the protagonists to rely on each other, building trust and affection through shared experiences. Their love story wouldn't be nearly as compelling without the constant threats and challenges they face together. The success of both the books and television adaptation proves that audiences crave stories where love blooms in the midst of chaos.

The marriage of action and romance requires careful attention to pacing, as demonstrated in Suzanne Collins' "The Hunger Games" trilogy. The relationship between Katniss Everdeen and Peeta Mellark evolves through moments of intense action, quiet reflection, and life-or-death situations. Their love story develops organically through shared trauma and triumph, making it feel authentic rather than forced. The way Collins weaves romantic elements into the action serves as a masterclass in maintaining tension on multiple levels. The constant threat of death adds weight to every romantic gesture and conversation. Their relationship becomes both a source of strength and vulnerability, raising the stakes of every dangerous situation.

James Cameron's "Titanic" (1997) provides another excellent example of how to structure an action-romance narrative, even when the audience knows the ultimate fate of the setting. The love story between Jack and Rose develops against the backdrop of impending disaster, with class conflicts and social constraints creating initial tension. The first half of the film focuses on character development and romantic connection, while the second half transforms into a survival story where their love is tested by catastrophic events. The film's structure demonstrates how to balance intimate character moments with spectacular action sequences. Each element serves to enhance the other, creating a more powerful overall narrative.

Consider how "The Mummy" (1999) uses humor, action, and romance to create a perfectly balanced adventure story. The relationship between Rick O'Connell and Evelyn Carnahan develops naturally through their shared quest, with both characters bringing different strengths to their partnership. Their witty banter and growing attraction provide relief from intense action sequences while maintaining narrative momentum. The film demonstrates how to use action scenes to reveal character traits that make your protagonists more attractive to each other. Their relationship feels earned because we see them face challenges together, support each other's growth, and discover mutual respect through shared adventures.

Examining Nora Roberts's romantic suspense novels reveals how to maintain romantic tension while building complex action plots. Her books often feature protagonists whose professional lives directly contribute to the danger they face, creating organic conflicts that test their developing relationships. Roberts excels at creating characters whose skills and weaknesses complement each other, making their partnership feel necessary for survival. Her work demonstrates how to use professional expertise as a source of attraction between characters. The technical details of their work add authenticity to the action while providing opportunities for characters to admire each other's competence.

The "Mission: Impossible" film series shows how to sustain romantic subplots across multiple installments while maintaining focus on action-driven narratives. Ethan Hunt's relationships are complicated by his dangerous profession, creating natural conflicts that feel authentic to the story world. The films demonstrate how to use romantic elements to humanize an action hero without diminishing their capability. Personal relationships raise the stakes of dangerous missions by giving the protagonist more to lose. The series also shows how to handle romantic tension when characters must prioritize duty over personal desires.

"Mr. & Mrs. Smith" (2005) provides an excellent example of how to integrate action and romance when both protagonists are equally capable. The film demonstrates how to use action sequences to explore relationship dynamics and create sexual tension. Their professional rivalry adds complexity to their romantic relationship while driving the plot forward. The action scenes serve as metaphors for their marital conflicts, making the violence meaningful on multiple levels. Their shared profession creates both conflict and common ground, demonstrating how to use character backgrounds to enhance both action and romance.

Linda Howard's romantic suspense novels offer valuable lessons in balancing detailed action sequences with emotional depth. Her books often feature protagonists who must work together despite initial mistrust or antagonism, creating rich opportunities for character development. Howard excels at writing physically capable heroines whose strength doesn't diminish their femininity or emotional vulnerability. Her work demonstrates how to write action scenes from a female perspective while maintaining romantic tension. The technical accuracy of her action sequences adds credibility to her stories while providing opportunities for characters to demonstrate their expertise.

The success of "Wonder Woman" (2017) shows how to craft a compelling action-romance narrative with a female protagonist. Diana's relationship with Steve Trevor develops naturally through their shared mission, with both characters maintaining their agency and importance to the plot. Their romance enhances rather than detracts from the action-driven narrative. The film demonstrates how to write love scenes that feel earned within the context of an action story. Their relationship provides emotional stakes that make the action sequences more meaningful.

Sandra Brown's extensive bibliography provides numerous examples of how to structure action-romance plots effectively. Her novels often begin with a catalyzing event that forces the protagonists together, creating immediate tension and conflict. Brown excels at maintaining suspense while developing believable romantic relationships between characters with opposing goals. Her work demonstrates how to use multiple points of view to build tension in both action and romantic scenes. The pacing of her novels shows how to balance quiet character moments with intense action sequences.

The enduring popularity of "Indiana Jones" films demonstrates how to maintain romantic subplots across action-heavy narratives. Indy's relationships are complicated by his adventurous lifestyle but never overshadow the main plot. The films show how to use romantic elements to humanize an action hero while maintaining their mystique. The relationships provide emotional context for the action sequences while adding depth to the character. The series demonstrates how to write romance that appeals to both male and female audiences.

"Pearl Harbor" (2001) shows how to handle complex romantic relationships within a historical action context. The love triangle between Rafe, Danny, and Evelyn creates emotional stakes that make the historical action more personally meaningful. Their relationships are tested by duty, loyalty, and extraordinary circumstances. The film demonstrates how to use historical events to create natural conflicts between characters. The action sequences gain emotional weight because we care about the characters' relationships.

"Casino Royale" (2006) provides a masterclass in writing sophisticated action-romance that appeals to modern audiences. Bond's relationship with Vesper Lynd adds emotional depth to his character while maintaining the sophistication expected of the franchise. Their romance feels authentic because it grows from mutual respect and attraction rather than mere physical chemistry. The film shows how to write intelligent dialogue that builds romantic tension while advancing the plot. Their relationship raises the stakes of the action while revealing important character traits.

The success of Kresley Cole's paranormal romance series demonstrates how to blend action, romance, and supernatural elements effectively. Her books feature complex world-building that creates natural sources of conflict between protagonists. Cole excels at writing action sequences that showcase both characters' abilities while building romantic tension. Her work shows how to use supernatural elements to create unique challenges for relationships. The physical dangers her characters face serve to accelerate emotional intimacy without feeling contrived.

1

———

EXPLORING THE FUSION OF GENRES

Emotional Depth

Emotional depth is the essential glue that binds the action and romance elements of an action & adventure romance novel. It connects readers profoundly with characters, transforming thrilling events into journeys of personal discovery and emotional resonance. In this genre, stakes are physical and deeply personal, captivating readers and making them invest in the characters' survival and relationships.

Strong lead characters must exhibit relatable flaws and personal struggles to achieve emotional depth. These imperfections make them human. For instance, a skilled adventurer protagonist may grapple with a fear of failure stemming from a past trauma. This fear can manifest in moments of hesitation during high-stakes scenarios, adding tension to action scenes. Readers will root for this character not only because of their bravery but also because they can see themselves in their vulnerabilities.

Deep point-of-view writing immerses readers in the characters' internal conflicts and feelings. The narrative becomes a window into their soul by delving into the protagonist's thoughts and emotions. For example, when faced with a life-threatening challenge, a character might reflect on a tender moment shared with their love interest. This heightens the tension of the action sequence and deepens the emotional stakes, allowing readers to feel their anxiety and determination.

Showcasing a range of relatable emotions—fear, joy, heartbreak—enriches the story. When the romantic relationship faces turmoil due to external pressures, such as a ticking clock to save a loved one or a betrayal from a trusted ally, the emotional fallout can lead to powerful scenes of conflict and reconciliation. A heated argument between the protagonists might reveal their insecurities, forcing them to confront their feelings for each other and their fears. This moment of vulnerability can be a pivotal turning point in the story, allowing both characters to grow.

The balance between emotional moments and action pacing is crucial. Quieter scenes, where characters reflect on their feelings or share intimate conversations, provide necessary respite from adrenaline-fueled sequences. For example, after a harrowing escape, a shared moment under the stars can serve as a backdrop for confessions of love, fears, and dreams for the future. This juxtaposition of high-stakes action and tender romance creates a rich tapestry that engages readers on multiple levels.

Ultimately, emotional depth enhances the stakes of action sequences and romantic developments. It transforms the narrative from a simple adventure into a story of personal growth and connection, ensuring that readers are not just spectators but participants in the characters' journeys. By weaving together the threads of action and emotion, authors can create a compelling narrative that resonates long after the final page is turned.

Compelling Romance

In the action & adventure romance genre, the romantic element is not merely an accessory; it is the heart of the narrative that infuses life into high-stakes scenarios. A compelling romantic relationship offers emotional depth and connection, allowing readers to invest in the characters' journeys amid thrilling escapades.

At the core of a captivating romance lies the natural chemistry between the protagonists. This chemistry should develop organically through shared experiences, moments of vulnerability, and authentic dialogue. Imagine a scene where two characters, trapped in a perilous situation—perhaps narrowly escaping an enemy stronghold—find solace in each other's presence. As they catch their breath, their eyes lock, and in that fleeting moment, the adrenaline rush transforms into a deeper bond. These small yet significant interactions lay the groundwork for their evolving relationship.

As the romance unfolds, showcasing the characters' vulnerabilities and strengths is essential. Their reactions to external pressures, such as life-threatening situations or moral dilemmas, can illustrate this progression. If one character faces the choice of saving their love interest or completing a mission, the resulting conflict heightens both the action stakes and the emotional weight of their relationship. Readers should witness how these choices reveal their true natures, fostering growth and connection.

Conflicts within the romantic relationship should arise realistically, often stemming from the characters' struggles or the chaos. Imagine a scenario in which the protagonists are separated during a high-octane chase. The distance creates physical tension and emotional turmoil as each grapples with feelings of fear and longing. This separation can lead to introspective moments where they confront their emotions, enriching the reader's understanding of their connection.

Balancing romantic moments with action is crucial. Quieter scenes are necessary respites, allowing for character development and deeper emotional engagement. After a climactic battle, a scene where the characters share a quiet meal under the stars can starkly contrast the chaos they've just endured. In this moment, they can reflect on their experiences, share their dreams, and express their fears, thus solidifying their bond. This contrast enhances the emotional stakes and makes the action sequences more impactful as readers become invested in the characters' well-being.

Ultimately, a compelling romance in an action & adventure narrative revolves around creating relatable characters who navigate the complexities of love amidst danger. The emotional connection should feel genuine, allowing readers to root for their union. By weaving together moments of intimacy, conflict, and growth, writers can craft a romance that resonates deeply, enriching the narrative and leaving a lasting impression. In this genre, romance is not just a subplot but an integral part of the adventure, transforming thrilling escapades into profound journeys of personal discovery and connection.

High-Stakes Action

In the realm of action & adventure romance, high-stakes action serves as the heartbeat of the narrative, driving both plot and character development. This genre thrives on adrenaline-fueled scenarios that captivate readers and immerse them in a world where danger lurks at every corner. The essence of high-stakes action lies in its ability to create tension and urgency, compelling characters to confront their fears and make pivotal choices.

High-stakes action is characterized by intense scenarios that physically, emotionally, and psychologically challenge protagonists. These situations can manifest in various forms, from perilous chases through bustling city streets to life-threatening confrontations in remote wildernesses. Imagine a scene where the protagonist, a skilled archaeologist, races against time to escape a collapsing ancient temple. The walls crumble around her as she clutches a priceless artifact. The urgency of the moment not only propels the plot forward but reveals her determination and resourcefulness, showcasing her character growth amid chaos.

High-stakes action is most effective when intricately woven into the fabric of the plot. Each action sequence should serve a dual purpose: advancing the story and deepening character development. Consider a scenario where the protagonist and her love interest are ambushed by mercenaries while attempting to retrieve a stolen treasure. Their partnership is tested as they fight for their lives, revealing underlying tensions and mutual reliance. The physical danger they face forces them to confront their feelings for one another, creating a compelling blend of action and romance that keeps readers engaged.

Action scenes must be vividly described and well-choreographed to captivate readers. Sensory details can transport readers into the heart of the action, allowing them to feel the rush of adrenaline and the weight of impending danger. Descriptions like "thundering footsteps echoing in the narrow alley" or "the sharp tang of gunpowder mixing with the salty sea breeze" create an immersive atmosphere that draws readers into the scene.

Additionally, the stakes of the action should escalate throughout the narrative, pushing characters to their limits and revealing their true natures. This escalation can be achieved through increasing external conflicts, such as a ticking clock or an impending disaster, that force characters to make critical decisions. For example, a protagonist may choose between saving a loved one or completing a mission that could prevent a greater catastrophe. Such dilemmas heighten tension and deepen the emotional stakes of the narrative, making the reader invested in the outcome.

High-stakes action is a vital component of an action & adventure romance, both as a catalyst for plot progression and a vehicle for character growth. By Writing intense, well-paced action sequences that resonate emotionally, writers can create a thrilling experience that keeps readers on the edge of their seats. The key lies in balancing these action elements with the emotional depth of the characters, ensuring that each pulse-pounding moment contributes to a richer, more satisfying narrative. As readers journey through the highs and lows of the protagonists' adventures, they witness exhilarating escapades and become deeply connected to the characters' struggles, triumphs, and blossoming romances.

2

CRAFTING COMPELLING LEAD CHARACTERS

Character Development: The Protagonist

Creating a compelling protagonist is essential to any best-selling action and adventure romance novel. The protagonist serves as the lens through which readers experience the story, so they must be relatable, dynamic, and richly developed. A well-crafted protagonist propels the plot forward and engages readers emotionally, encouraging them to invest in the character's journey.

Backstory: The Foundation of Depth

A captivating backstory is vital for the protagonist, providing the depth and context necessary for their actions and motivations. Consider Clara, a skilled archaeologist whose career is fueled by a childhood fascination with ancient civilizations sparked by her late father's adventurous tales. Clara's formative experiences, including her father's untimely death and her struggle for recognition in a male-dominated field, shape her worldview and drive her desire to uncover the truth behind a legendary artifact. These layers of complexity make her relatable and create a solid foundation for the plot.

Relatable Flaws and Strengths

A successful protagonist must embody relatable flaws and strengths that resonate with readers. Clara, for instance, is fiercely independent yet struggles with a deep fear of failure and a longing for acceptance. These vulnerabilities render her more human, allowing readers to empathize with her struggles. By showcasing her imperfections, such as her tendency to push people away when overwhelmed, writers can craft a character that readers root for, hoping she overcomes her internal battles.

Establishing Clear Motivations

Clear motivations are crucial for maintaining reader engagement. Clara's primary goal is to find the artifact her father devoted his life to discovering. This quest for closure propels her actions throughout the narrative, whether racing against a rival archaeologist or navigating treacherous terrains. With specific goals in mind, Clara's journey becomes purposeful, creating tension as she confronts obstacles that challenge her resolve.

Character Growth: The Arc of Transformation

Character growth is integral to a protagonist's journey. Throughout the story, Clara should learn from her experiences, evolving in response to her challenges. As she confronts dangers—whether from treasure hunters or emotional turmoil stemming from her past—she begins to grasp the importance of collaboration and trust. This growth arc resonates with readers, who witness Clara transforming from a solitary figure into a more open and connected individual.

Agency: An Active Protagonist

An active protagonist empowers the narrative. Clara should take initiative and make choices that drive the plot forward. Instead of waiting for rescue during a perilous moment, she could devise a clever escape plan, showcasing her resourcefulness and determination. This agency enriches her character and keeps readers engaged as they follow her proactive approach to overcoming challenges.

In summary, the protagonist is the heart of the action & adventure romance. By developing a rich backstory, relatable flaws, clear motivations, and a significant growth arc, writers can create a protagonist that resonates deeply with readers. Clara's journey, filled with external and internal conflicts, embodies what makes a character compelling and memorable in this dynamic genre.

Character Development: The Love Interest

In an action & adventure love story, the love interest is not merely a supporting character; they are an essential counterpart to the protagonist, endowed with their depth, motivations, and arcs. This complexity enriches the narrative, fostering a dynamic interplay between the leads that captivates readers and heightens romantic tension. Here, we will explore how to craft a compelling love interest that complements the protagonist, nurtures chemistry, and contributes meaningfully to the story.

Depth and Individuality

To fully engage readers, the love interest must be a fully realized individual, not just a romantic accessory. This involves providing them with a rich backstory, distinct personality traits, and their goals and conflicts. For instance, if the protagonist is a daring treasure hunter driven by adventure, the love interest could be a brilliant archaeologist passionate about preserving history. Their differing perspectives create tension and synergy as they navigate their motivations while working towards a common goal.

Consider Eliza, an aspiring botanist swept into a perilous journey alongside a rugged explorer. Eliza's desire to document rare plant species clashes with the explorer's reckless pursuit of fortune. Their contrasting motivations deepen their relationship and act as a catalyst for growth as both characters learn to appreciate each other's passions throughout their adventure.

Complementary Skills

A well-crafted love interest should possess complementary skills that enhance the narrative and foster a sense of partnership. This dynamic allows both characters to contribute meaningfully to overcoming challenges, showcasing their strengths while highlighting their vulnerabilities. For example, if the protagonist excels in physical strength and quick decision-making, the love interest could be skilled in strategy and negotiation, creating a balance that propels the plot forward.

Imagine a scenario where the skilled fighter protagonist faces a formidable enemy. With their diplomacy expertise, the love interest devises a plan to outsmart the antagonist rather than confront them directly. This collaboration enriches their relationship and underscores the importance of teamwork, demonstrating how their differences can lead to success.

Building Natural Chemistry

The natural chemistry between the lead and the love interest is crucial for establishing an authentic romantic connection. This chemistry can be cultivated through shared experiences, mutual respect, and organic dialogue that reveals attraction and emotional connection. Readers should feel the spark between the characters, making their relationship believable.

For instance, consider a scene where the protagonist and love interest find themselves trapped in a cave during a daring escape. As they work together to find a way out, their banter reveals their personalities—witty exchanges highlighting their differences while showcasing their growing attraction. These moments of levity amidst high-stakes situations allow readers to witness the evolution of their relationship, deepening their emotional investment.

Individual Character Arc

The love interest should also have its own character arc that allows for growth and change throughout the plot. Their journey should parallel or intersect with the protagonist's, creating tension and depth in the narrative. This dual arc strengthens the characters' bond and enriches the plot.

Consider a love interest who initially appears confident but gradually reveals insecurities from past failures. As the story progresses, the love interest confronts these fears, drawing strength from their relationship with the protagonist. This arc adds layers to the character and reinforces the theme of personal growth through love and partnership.

In adding a love interest to your story, you must make your character stand on their own with depth, complexity, and a meaningful arc. You can create a compelling romantic partnership that resonates with readers by ensuring they possess complementary skills, building natural chemistry, and allowing for individual growth. This relationship enhances the emotional stakes of your story and elevates the overall narrative, making it a memorable and engaging experience.

Supporting Characters: Adding Depth

In an action & adventure romance, supporting characters play a pivotal role in enriching the narrative. They are not mere background figures but integral to the story, providing distinct perspectives, emotional layers, and meaningful interactions that enhance the protagonists' journeys. A well-crafted supporting character can elevate the stakes, challenge the leads, and contribute to the overall depth of the narrative.

To create compelling supporting characters, they must possess distinct personalities that set them apart from the protagonist and love interest. Consider a mentor figure who embodies wisdom and experience, contrasting with the impulsive nature of the hero. This mentor might have their backstory—a past filled with failures and successes that inform their guidance. Imagine a retired spy who has witnessed the darker sides of the world, instilling caution and strategic thinking as a protagonist as he/she encounters treacherous situations. This character provides insight and serves as a moral compass, helping the hero grapple with their decisions.

Each supporting character should have a clear role in the story, serving a meaningful and integrated purpose. A character who provides comic relief can lighten the tension during intense moments, while a rival can introduce conflict that propels the protagonists to grow. For example, a rival treasure hunter motivated by greed could be an antagonist, pushing the hero and their love interest to confront their values and desires. Their interactions can lead to thrilling confrontations, heightening the stakes and adding complexity to the romantic dynamics.

Moreover, meaningful connections to the main characters enhance the story's emotional depth. Supporting characters should have relationships with the protagonist and love interest that reflect loyalty, conflict, or friendship. A best friend who stands by the protagonist through thick and thin can provide a sounding board for their inner struggles, adding humor and warmth. Consider a character who has known the protagonist since childhood; their shared history creates a rich backdrop for dialogue and interaction. This character might voice concerns about the protagonist's reckless decisions, grounding the narrative in relatable emotional stakes.

Authenticity is crucial in character development, and avoiding stereotypes is essential for creating multi-dimensional supporting characters. Each supporting character should have their motivations, desires, and complexities. A female sidekick, for instance, should not merely serve as a romantic interest or a damsel in distress; instead, she could be an expert in martial arts, capable of holding her own in a fight while also facing her challenges. By steering clear of clichés, writers can craft characters that resonate with readers, making the world feel lived-in and vibrant.

Supporting characters are vital to the success of an action & adventure romance. They should deepen the plot by influencing the protagonists' journeys, providing insights, and presenting challenges contributing to character growth and thematic exploration. By ensuring that each supporting character is distinct, purposeful, and authentic, writers can create a rich narrative landscape that captivates readers and elevates the story. As you develop your characters, remember that they are not just there to support the leads; they are essential players in the unfolding drama, each with their arcs that intertwine with the central narrative, ultimately enhancing the emotional impact of your action & adventure romance.

3

CRAFTING HIGH-STAKES PLOTS

External Conflicts: Driving the Action

External conflicts are the driving force of the narrative, propelling the story and capturing the reader's attention. These conflicts can take various forms, including life-threatening situations, environmental challenges, and antagonistic forces that test the protagonist's abilities. Clear and substantial stakes create an atmosphere of urgency that motivates characters to act decisively.

Imagine a protagonist racing against time to prevent a catastrophic event, such as a natural disaster threatening a bustling city. The ticking clock heightens tension, compelling the protagonist to navigate obstacles while managing personal relationships. For example, while trying to save the city from an impending earthquake, they may also seek to reconcile with a love interest whose life is in jeopardy. This intertwining of external and internal conflicts drives the plot and deepens character development, allowing readers to witness their strengths, weaknesses, and potential for growth.

Effective external conflict does more than escalate action; it reveals the characters' true natures. Their responses reveal resilience, courage, and vulnerabilities as they confront physical dangers—whether a treacherous mountain climb, a high-speed chase through narrow streets, or a confrontation with a ruthless enemy. For instance, during a fierce storm at sea, a character might struggle to keep the boat afloat while protecting their love interest. In this scenario, battling the elements test their commitment to one another and forces them to confront their fears.

Moreover, the audience should feel the intensity of the action and its implications for the characters' journeys. A well-crafted external conflict can evoke a visceral response, drawing readers into the heart of the story. Picture a scene where the protagonist must defuse a bomb in a crowded marketplace. The palpable tension, heightened by the ticking timer, creates an urgent atmosphere, while the emotional stakes rise with thoughts of loved ones who might be caught in the blast. This blend of high-stakes action and emotional investment keeps readers on the edge of their seats, eager for the outcome.

External conflicts can encompass broader societal issues that resonate with readers in addition to immediate threats. For example, a narrative might explore themes of injustice or corruption, where the protagonist challenges a powerful organization exploiting vulnerable communities. As they navigate this treacherous landscape, the external conflict drives the action and illuminates the protagonist's moral compass, enriching their character arc.

Likewise, external conflicts should propel the narrative forward while intertwining with the characters' internal struggles, creating a rich tapestry of tension and emotional depth. By ensuring that the stakes are clear and substantial, writers can create an engaging experience that resonates with readers, leaving them eager to see how the story unfolds.

Internal Conflicts: Driving the Romance

Internal conflicts form the emotional backbone of the narrative, enriching the romantic elements and deepening character connections. These conflicts often arise from personal struggles, emotional barriers, or past traumas that shape how characters interact and form relationships. As external action intensifies, the emotional stakes must rise, ensuring the romance evolves alongside the plot.

Consider a protagonist grappling with trust issues stemming from past betrayal. This internal struggle may manifest as hesitance to open up to a love interest, creating tension in their interactions. For instance, imagine a scene where Sarah stands on the brink of revealing her feelings for Jack yet hesitates, haunted by memories of a previous deceitful relationship. This vulnerability heightens romantic tension and invites readers to empathize with her plight.

The internal struggles should mirror this intensity as external conflicts escalate—perhaps during a high-octane chase through Barcelona, where Sarah and Jack flee from an adversary. The urgency compels Sarah to confront her trust issues directly. The ticking clock amplifies the emotional stakes: can she learn to trust Jack amidst the chaos, or will her past continue to haunt her? This interplay between external and internal conflicts creates a rich tapestry of narrative tension, engaging readers on multiple levels.

Furthermore, the evolution of the romance should be intricately tied to the characters' internal struggles. Their vulnerabilities become more pronounced as they face external threats, revealing how fears and insecurities impact their romantic decisions. For example, after a harrowing escape, Sarah might finally confide in Jack about her past, leading to a breakthrough in their relationship. This moment of honesty deepens their connection and serves as a turning point in the narrative, showcasing the transformative power of vulnerability.

Utilizing a deep point of view and emotional truth is essential for conveying these internal conflicts authentically. By delving into characters' thoughts and feelings, writers can create a visceral experience for readers, allowing them to feel the weight of the characters' struggles. When Sarah reflects on her fear of being hurt again, her internal dialogue might reveal raw emotions: "What if Jack is just like him? What if I let my guard down and end up shattered again?" Such introspection enriches her character and invites readers to invest in her journey, making the eventual resolution of her internal conflict all the more rewarding.

In conclusion, internal conflicts are vital for driving romance in action & adventure narratives. By intertwining personal struggles with external stakes, writers can craft a compelling emotional arc that resonates with readers. As characters confront their fears, the stakes of their romance rise alongside the action, creating a dynamic interplay that keeps readers engaged and invested in their journey toward love.

Plot Layers: Increasing Stakes

Adding a multi-layered plot is often needed for a compelling plot. A well-structured narrative intertwines external action with internal romantic arcs, ensuring readers remain captivated and emotionally invested throughout the journey. The complexity of the plot enhances the excitement of the action and deepens the emotional stakes of the romance, creating a rich tapestry of conflict and resolution.

To effectively raise the stakes, it is vital to introduce complications that impact both the plot's action and the romantic relationship. Consider Sarah, a skilled archaeologist racing against time to uncover a hidden treasure linked to her late father's mysterious past. As she delves deeper, she discovers that a ruthless treasure hunter named Marcus is also seeking the treasure. The external conflict intensifies when Sarah learns that Marcus is not only a formidable adversary but also a former love interest whose betrayal left her heartbroken. This unexpected twist heightens both the action's intensity and the emotional stakes of their romance.

As the story unfolds, clear goals for both Sarah and Marcus must be established. Sarah aims to find the treasure before Marcus to honor her father's legacy and reclaim her self-worth. Meanwhile, driven by his demons, Marcus seeks redemption for past mistakes, adding depth to his character. The obstacles they face—treacherous landscapes, booby traps, and the looming threat of betrayal—challenge their desires and push them toward personal growth.

The interplay between external and internal conflicts is crucial. As Sarah navigates the jungle, her encounters with Marcus force her to confront unresolved feelings of anger and betrayal. Each confrontation is tense, revealing their shared history and lingering emotional scars. For instance, during a narrow escape from a collapsing cave, Sarah must rely on Marcus, leading to moments of vulnerability that challenge her trust. This propels the action and deepens their connection, making readers root for a reconciliation that feels both inevitable and hard-earned.

Furthermore, layering conflicts ensure that each plot element influences the other, creating a cohesive narrative with tight pacing. When an unexpected betrayal occurs—perhaps a trusted ally reveals themselves working with Marcus—the stakes rise significantly. This twist threatens Sarah's quest and forces both characters to reevaluate their loyalties and feelings for one another. The emotional fallout from this betrayal can lead to poignant moments of reflection and growth, allowing the characters to evolve in response to their circumstances.

As the climax approaches, the intertwined nature of these layers becomes even more pronounced. The final confrontation between Sarah and Marcus should culminate in their external and internal struggles. They may find themselves in a perilous situation where they must work together to escape a collapsing temple, forcing them to confront their past and the potential for a future together. This moment marks the peak of action, and resolving their internal conflicts can lead to a satisfying emotional payoff for the reader.

Increasing the stakes through multi-layered plotting enriches the narrative of an action & adventure romance. By intertwining external and internal conflicts, writers can create a dynamic story that thrills readers with heart-pounding action while resonating emotionally through the characters' journeys. This interconnectedness ensures that it feels earned and impactful when resolution arrives, leaving readers satisfied and eager for more.

4

***

CRAFTING AN ENGAGING SETTING

Authentic Locations: Enhancing the Story

The setting is not just a backdrop; it acts as an integral character that shapes the narrative and influences the protagonists' choices. Authentic locations ground your story, providing a sense of place that resonates with readers. By crafting rich, well-researched environments, you elevate the stakes of your plot and deepen the emotional connections between characters.

Consider the contrast between a protagonist navigating the frenetic energy of a bustling metropolis and one traversing the stark beauty of a desolate wilderness. The cityscape, alive with honking horns and the scents of street food, creates a vibrant atmosphere that mirrors the urgency of action. In contrast, with its expansive silence and rugged terrain, the wilderness evokes feelings of isolation and introspection, allowing for moments of character reflection amidst the chaos. Each setting presents unique challenges and opportunities that significantly impact the story's tone and pacing.

Incorporating specific environmental challenges can heighten tension and complicate action sequences. Imagine a chase scene through the narrow alleyways of Marrakech, where vibrant colors and intricate market patterns serve as both obstacles and hiding places. The heat of the Moroccan sun adds urgency, while the scent of spices contrasts sharply with the adrenaline-fueled pursuit. Such details immerse readers in the experience, making them feel like they are alongside the characters.

Utilizing real-life locations provides a sense of familiarity that enhances the reader's connection to the story. For instance, setting a pivotal scene in the historic streets of Paris, with its iconic architecture and romantic ambiance, evokes wonder and nostalgia. However, balancing authenticity with imaginative liberties is essential. For instance, you might create a fictional town inspired by a real place, allowing for creative freedom while maintaining a relatable foundation.

Weather can also serve as a narrative device that reflects the emotional landscape of your characters. A sudden downpour during a climactic moment can symbolize turmoil or uncertainty, while a clear, sunny day might represent hope and newfound love. By weaving these atmospheric details into your narrative, you create a multi-dimensional world that resonates with readers on both emotional and sensory levels.

By grounding your narrative in well-researched environments that reflect your characters' emotional stakes, you create a vivid and immersive reading experience. Whether it's the bustling streets of a city or the serene expanse of nature, the settings you choose will influence the plot and enrich the emotional depth of your characters' journeys.

Atmospheric Details: Immersing the Reader

Creating an engaging setting in an action & adventure romance goes beyond merely placing characters in a location; it involves crafting an atmosphere that envelops both characters and readers. Atmospheric details breathe life into the narrative, providing a sensory experience deepening emotional connections.

To transport readers into your story world, employ vivid sensory descriptions that engage all five senses. In a coastal chase scene, the scent of salt evokes urgency, while the sound of crashing waves creates a backdrop of chaos. Imagine a protagonist sprinting along a rocky shoreline, the wind whipping through their hair, the sharp tang of ocean spray mingling with adrenaline. Such details enhance the immediacy of the action and ground the reader in the environment, making them feel as if they are experiencing the thrill alongside the characters.

Consider the atmosphere of a dense forest during an intense escape. The crunch of leaves beneath the characters' feet amplifies tension, each snap echoing like a countdown to danger. Dappled sunlight filtering through the canopy creates an interplay of light and shadow, symbolizing the uncertainty of their journey. By immersing readers in these sensory experiences, you allow them to feel the weight of the environment on the characters' journeys, making every moment more poignant.

Atmospheric details can also reflect the characters' emotional states, adding layers of meaning to the narrative. A storm brewing on the horizon can foreshadow conflict or turmoil, while a clear sky might symbolize hope. For example, if your protagonist grapples with inner conflict regarding their budding romance, a sudden downpour could mirror their emotional struggle, forging a powerful connection between the setting and their feelings. This technique enriches storytelling and deepens reader engagement with the characters' arcs.

Incorporating local weather patterns or seasonal changes can further enhance the atmosphere. An autumn story with leaves turning vibrant shades of red and gold evokes nostalgia and beautifully contrasts with high-stakes action. Conversely, a winter setting, with its biting cold and blanketing snow, amplifies feelings of isolation, particularly if characters face external threats.

Ultimately, the goal of atmospheric details is to create a multi-dimensional world that feels real and lived-in. By weaving together sensory descriptions, emotional resonance, and environmental reflections, you build a setting that supports the action and romance while becoming a character in its own right. Readers will find themselves observing the story and experiencing it, fully immersed in the sights, sounds, and sensations of the world you've crafted. This level of engagement is crucial for an action & adventure romance, where high stakes and deep emotions ensure that readers remain captivated until the very last page.

Cultural Elements: Adding Depth

The setting also serves as a vibrant character that influences the narrative's trajectory and the characters' experiences. Integrating cultural elements is one of the most powerful ways to enrich this setting. By weaving local customs, traditions, and societal norms into your story, you create a multi-dimensional world that resonates with readers and offers profound context for character motivations and interactions.

Imagine a romance blossoming amidst the vibrant chaos of a cultural festival. Picture a daring archaeologist named Maya in Mexico during the Day of the Dead celebrations. The streets are alive with colorful papel picado, the air thick with the aroma of pan de muerto, and the sounds of mariachis fill the night. This setting enhances the romantic tension between Maya and her love interest, a local historian named Javier while highlighting the clash between their differing backgrounds. As they navigate the festival together, sharing laughter and stories, they confront the complexities of their cultural differences, creating a rich tapestry of emotional depth that draws readers into their journey.

Understanding the historical context of a location can significantly inform character backstories and plot intricacies. Setting a story in Istanbul, a city steeped in a confluence of cultures and histories, provides a stunning backdrop. The protagonist, perhaps a resourceful treasure hunter named Alex, could be on a quest to uncover an ancient artifact hidden within the Hagia Sophia. As Alex delves deeper into the city's past, he encounters the physical challenges of his adventure and the cultural significance of the places he explores. The historical richness of Istanbul—its Byzantine and Ottoman influences, bustling bazaars, and enigmatic architecture—becomes integral to the plot, offering layers of meaning that enhance both action and romance.

Incorporating cultural elements also invites opportunities for conflict and character growth. A love story set against the backdrop of a traditional Indian wedding can explore themes of familial expectations and personal desires. As protagonists Aisha and Raj navigate the colorful chaos of the celebrations, they confront their fears and insecurities, ultimately learning to balance their love with the weight of their cultural obligations. This dynamic elevates the stakes of their romance and allows for a deeper exploration of identity and belonging, making the setting essential to their journey.

Consider the details that bring cultural elements to life to immerse readers fully in your story. Describing the intricate patterns of a traditional garment, the rhythm of a local dance, or the significance of a ritual creates vivid imagery that resonates emotionally. For instance, the sight of a couple exchanging garlands during a wedding ceremony symbolizes their commitment and love as a poignant reminder of the traditions shaping their lives.

By thoughtfully integrating cultural elements into your action & adventure romance, you enhance the authenticity of your setting and create a richer, more engaging narrative. Readers will be drawn to the high-stakes action and thrilling adventures and the emotional depth and complexity arising from the characters' interactions with their cultural surroundings. In doing so, you create a world that feels alive and relevant, inviting readers to lose themselves in the journey of love and adventure.

5
____

BALANCING ACTION AND ROMANCE: A DELICATE DANCE

Pacing Techniques: Mixing Intensity Levels

in an action & adventure romance, balancing heart-pounding action with tender moments is essential for maintaining reader engagement. This interplay of pacing heightens emotional stakes and allows readers to immerse themselves in the characters' journeys. By alternating high-energy sequences with quieter, character-driven interactions, writers can establish a rhythm that keeps readers invested in both action and romance.

One effective technique is using short, punchy sentences during action scenes. This rapid-fire delivery mirrors urgency, propelling readers through chases, fights, and narrow escapes. For example, in a scene where the protagonist flees from an enemy: "She dashed down the alley. Heart racing. Breath coming in quick bursts." Such sentences convey urgency and immerse readers in the frantic pace of the chase. Concise descriptions and active verbs amplify intensity, drawing readers into the action.

Incorporating sensory details can further enrich action scenes. Vividly describing sounds, sights, and physical sensations creates a more immersive experience. Picture two characters in a fierce battle: the sharp clang of metal, the whoosh of a sword slicing through the air, and the gritty feel of dirt beneath their feet all contribute to a vivid tableau that transports readers into the heart of the conflict. These sensory elements heighten stakes and make the action feel immediate and real.

Character reactions during high-stakes moments are equally crucial. Readers want to see how characters respond to danger, which drives the plot and deepens emotional connections. As the protagonist narrowly escapes a life-threatening situation, their feelings of fear, determination, and vulnerability should be laid bare. Describing a character's trembling hands or pounding heart adds emotional depth, allowing readers to empathize with their plight.

Transitioning from action to romance requires a thoughtful approach to scene structure. Each scene should have a clear purpose—advancing the plot, developing character relationships, or building tension. For action scenes, this means escalating stakes as the narrative progresses. A well-structured fight might start with minor obstacles, such as grappling with an enemy, before culminating in a major confrontation that tests the characters' limits. This gradual increase in tension creates a satisfying arc that keeps readers on edge.

Conversely, quieter scenes are vital for character development. These moments allow for deeper exploration of emotions and relationships, providing necessary counterbalance to adrenaline-fueled action. A simple dinner conversation can reveal backstory, motivations, and nuances of characters' relationships, contrasting sharply with recent chaos. This juxtaposition enriches the narrative and reinforces emotional stakes.

Transitions between scenes also play a critical role in maintaining momentum. A smooth shift from an intense battle to a moment of reflection or tenderness can create powerful emotional impact. For instance, after a harrowing escape, a character might find solace in their love interest's arms, allowing for vulnerability that beautifully contrasts with previous chaos. This interplay between action and romance keeps readers engaged, eagerly anticipating what comes next.

Mastering pacing techniques that mix intensity levels is pretty fundamental. By alternating between gripping action and intimate moments, writers create a narrative that resonates deeply with readers. Each scene must serve a purpose, whether escalating tension or deepening emotional connections, ultimately culminating in a cohesive story that captivates from start to finish.

Scene Structure: Establishing Purpose

Every scene must serve a distinct purpose that propels the narrative forward—advancing the plot, deepening character relationships, or building tension. Clarity in purpose is essential for maintaining a satisfying flow and keeping readers engaged in the characters' journeys.

Action scenes should escalate in stakes, leading to thrilling and earned climaxes. A well-structured fight sequence may begin with minor obstacles, such as dodging henchmen's attacks, before culminating in a confrontation with the main antagonist. This gradual increase in tension keeps readers on edge and allows them to witness characters' growth as they face formidable challenges. For instance, in a chase through a bustling marketplace, protagonists might initially evade capture by weaving through stalls, but as tension builds, they find themselves cornered, forced to rely on their wits and teamwork to escape.

Conversely, quieter scenes are equally vital for character development. These moments provide breathing space for emotional exploration and relationship building. A dinner conversation following a harrowing escape can poignantly contrast with the preceding chaos, revealing the characters' vulnerabilities and motivations. Imagine protagonists sharing a candlelit meal, the flickering light casting dancing shadows as they recount their fears and dreams. This intimate setting allows readers to connect with characters personally, understanding their emotional landscapes amidst external turmoil.

Transitions between action and romance scenes are crucial for maintaining momentum. A seamless shift enhances the emotional impact of both types of scenes. After an intense battle, following characters as they find solace in each other's arms can create a powerful juxtaposition. The adrenaline of the fight lingers, yet in this quiet moment, they reflect on what they've fought for, deepening their bond and reinforcing relationship stakes.

Whether brimming with action or steeped in romance, each scene should contribute to the overarching narrative. By establishing clear purposes for each moment, writers create a cohesive experience that captivates readers from start to finish. This balance enriches the story and ensures emotional stakes resonate deeply, leaving readers eager to discover what unfolds next.

Character Development: Quiet Moments

In the fast-paced world of action & adventure romance, quiet moments may seem like mere pauses in the action, yet they are vital for character development. These moments allow characters to reflect on their experiences, solidifying their emotional journeys and adding depth to their personalities. A well-placed quiet scene can transform a thrilling narrative into a deeply resonant story that lingers in the reader's mind long after the final page.

Quiet moments create space for characters to explore vulnerabilities and fears. After a harrowing escape from a collapsing building, the two protagonists might be isolated in a secluded cabin. The adrenaline fades as they catch their breath, and the weight of their experiences settles. This becomes the perfect opportunity for them to share thoughts, revealing insecurities masked by chaos. One character might express a fear of losing loved ones, while the other admits to a history of abandonment. Such revelations enhance character depth and forge a stronger emotional connection.

Building chemistry during these quieter scenes is essential for engaging readers. Natural dialogue serves as a vehicle for intimacy, allowing characters to connect on a deeper level. Imagine a scene where protagonists share a meal after a long day of conflict. As they prepare dinner together, playful banter ensues, revealing their personalities and shared history. The clinking of dishes and aroma from cooking creates an atmosphere inviting closeness, while laughter over a cooking mishap deepens their bond. These moments of levity remind readers of the humanity and warmth that can exist even amidst turmoil.

Progressive intimacy should be depicted realistically, reflecting relationships' challenges in high-stakes environments. Characters may encounter misunderstandings or external threats testing their connection. After a narrow escape from danger, one character might feel the urge to distance themselves, fearing their loved one might be hurt. This conflict can lead to a poignant scene where they confront their fears, resulting in vulnerability that ultimately strengthens their relationship. Resolving such conflicts should feel earned, showcasing characters' growth and commitment.

Meaningful moments crafted with intention resonate with readers emotionally. Consider a quiet scene where characters share dreams and aspirations while stargazing on a rooftop after a day of intensity. As they gaze at the night sky, they might discuss hopes for the future, revealing layers of their personalities that were previously hidden. This moment of connection enriches their relationship and allows readers to invest in their journey, rooting for their success in action and romance.

Balancing action and romance requires careful attention to pacing and character arcs. Quiet moments are not merely pauses in the narrative but essential tools for character development. Each scene should contribute to a cohesive narrative that captivates readers from start to finish. By allowing characters to reflect, connect, and grow in these moments, writers can create a rich tapestry of emotions that elevates their action & adventure romance.

6

———

CRAFTING THRILLING ACTION SCENES

Key Elements of Writing Action Scenes

Crafting compelling action scenes is a must for any writer in the romance genre. These scenes are pivotal moments that propel the plot, develop character relationships, and heighten emotional stakes. To create engaging and impactful action sequences, consider the following key elements.

Clear Choreography

The foundation of any action scene is its choreography. A well-structured sequence allows readers to follow the action without confusion, creating an immersive experience. Begin by mapping out the sequence of events. Visualize your characters' movements and the environment around them. For instance, if your protagonist is in a high-speed chase through a bustling market, detail their path—dodging vendors, weaving through crowds, and narrowly avoiding obstacles. Using precise language to describe these interactions helps readers visualize the scene vividly. Instead of saying, "She ran fast," you might write, "She sprinted past a fruit stall, her fingers grazing the oranges as she narrowly avoided a toppled crate." Such descriptions clarify the action and enhance the tension.

Sensory Details

Incorporating sensory details is crucial for immersing readers in the action. Engage all five senses to create a rich experience. Describe the sounds of the environment—perhaps the distant wail of police sirens or the thudding footsteps on cobblestones. Visual elements, like sunlight glinting off a blade or the shadow of an approaching enemy, heighten the stakes. Smells, such as acrid smoke or the metallic tang of blood, anchor readers in the scene. For example, when a character dodges a bullet, illustrate not only the action but the auditory experience: "The bullet whizzed past her ear, a sharp hiss that filled her with adrenaline, as the rush of air brushed against her skin." This detail creates urgency and draws readers deeper into the narrative.

Emotional Impact

Action scenes should evoke emotions that resonate with readers, connecting them to the characters' experiences. Utilizing a deep point of view amplifies this emotional impact. Rather than simply narrating the action, delve into the character's thoughts and feelings during intense moments. For instance, as a character faces a life-threatening situation, portray their fear and resolve: "Her heart raced, pounding like a drum in her chest, but she couldn't falter. Not now. Not when everything she loved was at stake." This internal dialogue allows readers to empathize with the character, heightening their investment in the outcome.

Realistic Consequences

An effective action scene must reflect realistic consequences. Characters should face tangible outcomes for their actions—physical injuries, emotional fallout, or relationship shifts. This adds depth to the narrative and makes the stakes feel genuine. If your protagonist narrowly escapes a deadly confrontation, consider the aftermath: Are they physically wounded? Do they grapple with guilt or trauma? For instance, after a fierce battle, a character might find themselves nursing a wound and haunted by the memory of a lost friend. This exploration of consequences enriches character development and keeps readers engaged.

Strategic Pacing

Pacing is crucial in maintaining reader engagement during action scenes. Varying the rhythm within these sequences amplifies tension and excitement. Use shorter sentences and paragraphs to quicken the pace during high-intensity moments, creating a sense of urgency. For example, in a climactic fight scene: "He lunged forward. A fist connected. She stumbled back. Gasping." This rapid-fire structure propels the reader through the action. Conversely, employ longer sentences for moments of reflection or tension buildup, allowing readers to catch their breath before the next wave of excitement. This rhythmic variation keeps readers on the edge of their seats.

Writing dynamic and engaging action scenes requires a careful balance of clear choreography, sensory details, emotional depth, realistic consequences, and strategic pacing. By focusing on these key elements, you can create action sequences that thrill and resonate emotionally with your readers, enhancing the overall impact of your story.

Technical Tips for Writing Action Scenes

Writing action scenes that captivate readers requires a thoughtful approach. Each scene should serve a clear purpose and contribute to the overall narrative, whether it's advancing the plot, deepening character relationships, or raising the stakes. Here are essential tips to consider when writing your action scenes.

Clear Goal

Before writing an action scene, identify its core objective. What do you want to achieve? Is it a pivotal moment that propels the protagonist into a new challenge, or a confrontation that tests a relationship? Establishing a clear goal ensures that every element of the scene contributes meaningfully to the story. For instance, in a chase sequence, the goal might be to escape a pursuing enemy, heightening tension and urgency. Each action taken by the characters should align with this objective, creating a cohesive and thrilling experience.

Rising Action

Building tension is crucial in action scenes; it creates anticipation that keeps readers engaged. Start with lower stakes or a hint of intrigue, gradually escalating conflicts as the scene unfolds. For example, if your protagonist is infiltrating a high-security facility, begin with small obstacles—perhaps a guard they must evade or a locked door to pick. As they progress, introduce greater challenges, such as an unexpected alarm or a confrontation with a rival. This rising action leads to a climax that feels earned and impactful.

Climax

The climax of your action scene should be the peak of tension and conflict, where stakes are highest. This moment is crucial to convey intensity to readers. For instance, in a dramatic showdown, the protagonist might face their nemesis, with the outcome affecting not just their fate but the lives of those they care about. Use vivid imagery and dynamic language to illustrate the chaos and urgency of this moment, ensuring readers are fully immersed.

Resolution

After the climax, provide a resolution that ties up the loose ends. This can include characters regrouping, assessing the aftermath, or facing new challenges that arise from the action. For example, if the protagonist narrowly escapes danger, the resolution might involve them reflecting on their choices or preparing for the next phase of their journey. This provides closure and sets the stage for further developments, maintaining reader interest.

Transition

Smooth transitions into and out of action scenes are vital for maintaining reader engagement. Use elements from preceding scenes to lead into the action, ensuring a seamless flow. For instance, if the action follows a tense conversation, describe the protagonist's racing heart as they step into the fray, creating a natural progression. Likewise, after the climax, transition back into quieter moments that allow for reflection and character development. This rhythmic variation keeps readers invested in the narrative.

By implementing these tips, you can create action scenes that not only thrill but also resonate with readers on a deeper level. Each scene will feel purposeful and impactful, contributing to the overall emotional arc of your story.

Remember, the goal is to immerse your audience in the experience, making them feel every pulse-pounding moment and every heart-stopping decision.

Emotional Impact

Writing action scenes that resonate emotionally with readers is essential for creating a memorable narrative. These scenes should not only thrill but also deepen the reader's connection to the characters and the storyline. To achieve this, writers must focus on several key aspects that elevate the emotional stakes during high-intensity moments.

Character Connection

Establishing a deep connection between readers and characters is the first step in ensuring emotional impact. Utilizing a close point of view allows readers to experience the characters' emotions in real-time, creating intimacy. For instance, when a protagonist faces a life-threatening situation, delve into their psyche. Illustrate their racing heart, the sweat trickling down their brow, and the thoughts spiraling through their mind—perhaps memories of loved ones or unfulfilled dreams. This exploration transforms a mere action sequence into a poignant moment that readers can relate to and remember.

Reader Experience

Every action scene should contribute to the overall emotional arc of the narrative. Consider a scene where a character must make a split-second decision to save a loved one. The tension builds as they weigh the risks, drawing the reader into their turmoil. By showcasing the character's fears, hopes, and motivations, the action becomes not just about survival but about the emotional stakes involved. This journey evokes empathy and investment from the reader, making the outcome feel significant.

Memorable Moments

To create lasting impressions, highlight key moments that elevate the action beyond physicality. For example, imagine a character who, during a fierce battle, suddenly recalls a promise made to a dying friend. This moment of clarity could lead them to fight with renewed vigor, turning the tide of the conflict. Such emotional breakthroughs enhance the action and provide depth to the character's journey, ensuring that readers remember these moments long after the adrenaline rush has faded.

Character Investment

Readers are more engaged in the action if they care about the characters involved. Build strong character arcs and relationships throughout the narrative so that when an action scene unfolds, the stakes feel personal. If a beloved character is in peril, the emotional weight of the scene intensifies. For instance, if a protagonist fights to save their partner, the reader's investment in that relationship amplifies the tension. The action then serves a dual purpose: it propels the plot forward while reinforcing the emotional bonds that have been developed.

Lasting Impact

Ultimately, the goal of action scenes is to create a lasting impact that resonates with readers. This can be achieved through character development, thematic elements, and the integration of emotional stakes. For example, consider a scene where a hero confronts a villain who embodies their greatest fear. The confrontation tests their physical abilities and forces them to confront inner demons. By intertwining physical and emotional battles, the scene becomes a powerful testament to character growth and resilience, leaving readers with a sense of catharsis.

Writing action scenes that evoke emotional responses is crucial for engaging readers on a deeper level. By focusing on character connection, enhancing the reader experience, crafting memorable moments, ensuring character investment, and aiming for lasting impact, writers can transform thrilling action sequences into profound narrative experiences. This emotional depth captivates readers and ensures that the action serves a purpose beyond mere entertainment, enriching the overall story.

7

CRAFTING HEARTFELT ROMANTIC SCENES

Building Chemistry

Creating a compelling romantic relationship within an action & adventure narrative hinges on the chemistry between characters. This chemistry is more than mere attraction; it's an intricate blend of emotions, dialogue, and shared experiences that immerse readers in the characters' world. Here's how to effectively build that chemistry.

Natural dialogue is the foundation of any relationship, providing insight into the characters' minds and hearts. It should flow organically, reflecting their unique personalities and backgrounds. For instance, if your protagonist is a witty, sarcastic adventurer, their banter with a serious love interest can create an engaging dynamic. Consider this exchange:

"Do you always jump into danger without a plan?" she asked, arching an eyebrow.

"Only when the plan is boring," he replied with a smirk, his eyes revealing more than just bravado.

This dialogue showcases their personalities while hinting at underlying attraction and tension. Distinctive speaking patterns highlight individuality, making each character memorable. Emotional truth is crucial; characters must express feelings that resonate with readers. If a character feels nervous or excited, let those emotions permeate their words and actions. For example, a character might fumble their words when addressing their crush, allowing readers to empathize with their vulnerability.

Physical attraction adds another layer of tension to the chemistry. Use sensory details to vividly describe their reactions to each other. For instance:

As she brushed past him, the scent of her jasmine perfume enveloped him, sending his heart racing. He felt the warmth radiating from her skin, and for a moment, the chaos of the world faded away.

These details enhance emotional stakes and create palpable tension that readers can feel. The physical connection should be seamlessly woven into the narrative, becoming integral to the characters' evolving relationship.

Building an emotional connection is essential for deepening chemistry. Focus on shared experiences that bring characters closer together, such as overcoming challenges, engaging in teamwork, or revealing personal stories. For example:

After narrowly escaping a collapsing bridge, they huddled beneath a tree, adrenaline coursing through their veins. "I thought we were done for," she admitted, her voice trembling.

"Yeah, me too," he replied, his gaze steady. "But we made it. Together."

This exchange reinforces their bond and establishes trust, showing how they open up to each other over time. Such moments of vulnerability allow characters to reveal their true selves, solidifying their connection and making the romance feel authentic.

Building chemistry in romance scenes involves Writing natural dialogue, emphasizing physical attraction, and fostering emotional connections. By focusing on these elements, you create a relationship that resonates with readers, drawing them into the heart of your action & adventure romance. The chemistry should feel electric, leaving readers eagerly turning pages to see how the relationship unfolds amid thrilling adventures.

Transitioning to World-Building

The setting of your romance is as crucial as the characters themselves. A well-crafted environment serves not only as a backdrop but also as a catalyst for emotional connection, enhancing intimacy. To achieve this, create rich, immersive locations that resonate with the narrative and the emotional stakes of the romance.

Begin by selecting locations that reflect your story's themes and emotions. For instance, if your protagonists navigate a treacherous mountain range, the harsh environment can mirror the challenges in their relationship. Conversely, a serene beach at sunset might symbolize peace and connection, contrasting with external conflicts. Each setting should amplify romantic tension and serve as a stage for pivotal moments.

Use specific, well-researched details to bring your locations to life. Describe the scent of pine trees in a forest, the sound of waves crashing on rocky shores, or the vibrant colors of a bustling market. These sensory details immerse readers in the world and evoke emotions that align with the characters' experiences. For example, as your characters share a quiet moment in a candle-lit café, the flickering light symbolizes the warmth of their growing bond, while the aroma of fresh coffee evokes comfort and intimacy.

Utilizing a deep point-of-view can significantly enhance the emotional impact of your romance scenes. This technique allows readers to experience the characters' feelings as if they were their own, forging a deeper connection to the narrative. When writing from a character's perspective, delve into their thoughts and sensations during key moments. For instance, when a character brushes against their love interest's hand for the first time, describe the warmth spreading through them, the quickening of their heartbeat, and the whirlwind of emotions accompanying this simple yet profound interaction.

Incorporate internal monologues that reveal the characters' vulnerabilities and desires. For example, as they navigate a thrilling escape from danger, one character might reflect on their growing feelings for the other, grappling with fear of loss and the exhilaration of newfound love. By intertwining their emotional journey with the physical setting, you create a rich tapestry that draws readers deeper into the story.

Ultimately, your goal is to take readers on an emotional journey that mirrors the highs and lows of the characters' relationship. As they experience moments of joy, tension, and vulnerability, the setting should evolve alongside them. For instance, a romantic encounter in a rain-soaked alley can symbolize chaos, while a quiet moment under a starlit sky might represent clarity and hope.

Ensure that the conclusion of your romance arc ties seamlessly into the resolution of external conflicts. As your characters face their final challenges, the setting can play a pivotal role in their emotional growth. Perhaps they return to the location of their first kiss, confronting their fears and solidifying their commitment. This not only provides closure but also leaves readers feeling fulfilled and invested in the characters' futures.

In Writing your romance scenes, remember that world-building is not just a backdrop but a living entity that interacts with your characters. By thoughtfully integrating setting, emotional depth, and reader experience, you create a powerful narrative that resonates long after the final page is turned.

Developing the Relationship

in an action & adventure romance, the evolution of the romantic relationship is as crucial as the high-stakes action driving the plot. A well-crafted romance should unfold naturally, reflecting the complexities of human emotions and the challenges faced by the characters. This exploration delves into creating a believable and engaging relationship between your protagonists, emphasizing progressive intimacy, realistic conflicts, genuine emotions, and meaningful moments.

Progressive Intimacy

The journey toward intimacy must unfold gradually. Begin with small, tender moments that establish a connection. Imagine a scene where the protagonists find themselves trapped in a cave after a daring escape. As they collaborate to find a way out, they might share fleeting touches—an accidental brush of hands while reaching for the same flashlight or a reassuring squeeze on the shoulder during moments of fear. These gestures signify the inception of their emotional and physical bond.

As the story unfolds, allow this intimacy to deepen. This could manifest through shared secrets—perhaps one character reveals a traumatic experience while the other responds with empathy. Such exchanges build trust and forge an authentic connection. Gradually introduce more intimate physical moments, like holding hands during quiet reflection or sharing a lingering gaze that conveys unspoken feelings. Each step should feel earned, reflecting the characters' growing emotions and vulnerabilities.

Realistic Conflicts

Every relationship faces challenges, and introducing realistic conflicts is essential for maintaining tension and engagement. Conflicts can arise from various sources, both external and internal. For instance, if your protagonists are on the run from a formidable adversary, the constant danger can strain their relationship. One character may feel compelled to protect the other, creating tension around their ability to keep each other safe.

Internal struggles are equally significant. Characters may grapple with insecurities or fears of commitment that threaten their blossoming romance. For example, one character might hesitate to open up due to a history of abandonment. Weaving these conflicts into the narrative creates stakes that resonate with readers, allowing them to empathize with the characters' struggles.

Genuine Emotions

Emotional authenticity is the cornerstone of a compelling romance. Avoid clichés and focus on the multifaceted nature of love. Characters should experience a spectrum of emotions—joy, jealousy, fear, and excitement—as they navigate their relationship. After a thrilling escape, they might share a moment of exhilaration that quickly turns to vulnerability as they confront their feelings.

Highlight the confusion that often accompanies attraction. One character may be drawn to the other yet fear the implications of their feelings amid chaos. This internal conflict can lead to poignant moments of reflection, allowing readers to witness the characters' emotional journeys. By portraying love as complex and sometimes tumultuous, you create a richer, more relatable narrative.

Meaningful Moments

Key moments in a relationship can define its trajectory and leave a lasting impact on both characters and readers. These moments should resonate emotionally. Consider a scene where the protagonists face a life-or-death scenario, and one character makes a sacrifice for the other. This act of bravery can serve as a turning point, solidifying their bond and illuminating the depth of their feelings.

Another significant moment might unfold during a quiet evening under the stars. As they share dreams and fears, they may lean closer, culminating in a kiss that feels both inevitable and charged with emotion. These meaningful interactions enhance the romantic arc and deepen the reader's investment in the characters' journey.

Developing a romantic relationship in an action & adventure narrative requires a delicate balance of progressive intimacy, realistic conflicts, genuine emotions, and meaningful moments. By focusing on these elements, you can create a relationship that feels authentic and engaging, drawing readers into the emotional landscape of your characters as they navigate the thrilling challenges of their adventure.

8

ESSENTIALS OF PLOT STRUCTURE

Opening Hook

The opening hook is essential for your action & adventure romance novel, setting the tone and engaging readers from the first page. It creates a vital first impression, designed to capture interest and draw readers into the story. In the fast-paced world of action & adventure romance, the opening hook must be particularly compelling, introducing a scenario or question that piques curiosity and propels readers forward.

To craft an effective opening hook, consider starting with a dynamic scene that hints at the high-stakes action to come. Imagine a protagonist, a skilled treasure hunter named Mia, racing against time to escape a collapsing ancient temple deep in the Amazon rainforest. The vivid imagery of crumbling stone and the roar of cascading water creates an immediate sense of urgency. As dust swirls around her, readers are introduced to Mia's peril and the adrenaline-pumping adventure that lies ahead. This kind of opening captures attention and establishes a tone of excitement and danger.

In addition to action, the opening hook should hint at the romantic tension that will develop throughout the story. Perhaps as Mia navigates her escape, she encounters Alex, a rival treasure hunter with whom she shares a complicated history. Their charged interactions, filled with unresolved feelings and competitive banter, set the stage for a romantic arc intertwined with the adventure. By introducing both action and romance, you create a multifaceted hook that promises a thrilling journey for readers.

Establishing the protagonist early on is crucial for fostering a connection with readers. They should empathize with Mia as she faces external dangers and internal dilemmas. What drives her? What fears does she harbor? Presenting her motivations—perhaps a quest to prove herself after a past failure—invites readers to invest emotionally in her journey. The goal is to make them feel they must continue reading to uncover what happens next, ensuring they are emotionally tethered to her fate from the very beginning.

Moreover, incorporating a compelling question or dilemma into your opening hook can elevate the stakes. This could be a moral choice that Mia faces as she decides whether to save Alex or continue her escape alone. Such a dilemma deepens the narrative, encouraging readers to ponder the implications of her decision.

The opening hook is your chance to create a captivating first impression. By blending high-stakes action with hints of romantic tension, establishing a relatable protagonist, and posing a compelling question, you can ensure readers are hooked from the very first page. This initial investment lays the foundation for the intricate dance of adventure and romance that will unfold throughout your novel.

Rising Action

The rising action serves as the backbone of your action & adventure romance, propelling the plot forward while deepening the emotional stakes. This phase encompasses most of your narrative, providing ample opportunity to escalate tension and develop characters. It intricately weaves together external conflicts—thrilling, high-stakes situations that keep readers on the edge of their seats—and internal conflicts that explore the characters' emotional journeys.

In an action & adventure romance, the protagonist's journey should resemble a thrilling rollercoaster, filled with obstacles that test their resolve and challenge their relationships. Imagine a heroine racing against time to uncover hidden treasure before a ruthless rival. As she navigates treacherous terrain, dodges traps, and deciphers ancient codes, she grapples with her growing attraction to her rugged, enigmatic partner, who harbors his own secrets. This duality of external and internal conflict creates a rich tapestry that captivates readers.

Introducing subplots that enhance the primary storyline is essential during this phase. Perhaps the heroine's initial mistrust of her partner leads to misunderstandings that complicate their budding romance. As they face physical dangers together—such as escaping a collapsing cave or evading capture—their emotional barriers begin to crumble. Each challenge heightens the stakes of their external quest and forces them to confront their feelings for one another. This interplay between action and romance keeps readers engaged, eager to see how the characters will evolve.

Complications in the romantic relationship are vital during this phase. A well-timed moment of vulnerability—like the hero sharing a painful memory—can deepen the emotional connection between the characters. This revelation might occur after a narrow escape, where adrenaline amplifies their emotions. The tension should be palpable, with stakes extending beyond physical survival to encompass the characters' hearts and their willingness to take risks for love.

As the rising action unfolds, maintaining a steady increase in tension is crucial. Each chapter should build upon the last, introducing new challenges that seem insurmountable. If the protagonists are on a quest for a mythical artifact, they might encounter increasingly difficult trials: deciphering a riddle, surviving a deadly ambush, or navigating a trap-filled labyrinth. These moments should be interspersed with quieter scenes that allow for character development, such as shared laughter over a campfire or heartfelt conversations about hopes and fears.

Ultimately, the rising action should culminate in a crescendo that leads seamlessly into the climax. By the time readers reach this pivotal moment, they should be fully invested in both the action and the romance. The stakes should be at their highest, with characters facing external threats and internal dilemmas that threaten to tear them apart. This blend of tension and emotional depth makes action & adventure romance compelling, ensuring readers are not only entertained but also deeply moved by the characters' journeys.

The rising action is where your story truly comes to life. It balances escalating external conflicts with intimate internal struggles. By intertwining thrilling adventures with poignant emotional moments, you will create a narrative that resonates with readers, drawing them deeper into the world you've crafted and leaving them eager for what comes next.

Climax

The climax of an action & adventure romance novel represents the narrative's emotional and action-packed peak, where the threads of conflict intertwine and reach their highest intensity. This pivotal moment transcends mere high-stakes action; it serves as a crucible that tests the characters' limits, compelling them to confront both external dangers and their internal struggles.

Crafting the climax requires balancing thrill and emotional resonance. The stakes must be at their zenith—both in the plot and the romantic arc. Picture a scenario where the protagonist, a fearless treasure hunter, has finally located a legendary artifact that holds the key to saving her homeland from impending doom. As she reaches for the artifact, she discovers that her love interest, a rival treasure hunter with whom she shares a tumultuous history, is also after the same prize. This moment amplifies not only the physical danger but also intensifies their emotional conflict.

During the climax, a relationship crisis often unfolds, forcing the characters to make pivotal choices that will define their arcs. It is here that the emotional stakes come to the forefront. Perhaps the protagonist must decide between claiming the artifact for herself or allowing her rival to take it, fully aware that doing so could lead to his downfall. This choice encapsulates the essence of their relationship—trust, betrayal, and the possibility of redemption. Readers should feel the weight of this decision, experiencing the tension arising from both the unfolding action and the emotional implications of the characters' choices.

To create an unforgettable climax, weave external and internal conflicts together seamlessly. The protagonist's journey should reflect not only the physical challenges she faces but also her growth and transformation as a character. If she has grappled with trusting others throughout the story, the climax should compel her to confront this flaw. Will she finally let go of her fears and trust her rival, or will she succumb to her insecurities, jeopardizing not only the mission but also their budding romance?

The events leading up to the climax should maximize tension and anticipation. Employ vivid imagery and dynamic action to keep readers on the edge of their seats. Imagine the sound of footsteps echoing in a dark cave, the flickering light of a torch illuminating ancient inscriptions, and the rush of adrenaline as the characters face off against rival treasure hunters or natural obstacles. This is the moment for heart-pounding action, where every second counts and every decision carries significant weight.

Ultimately, the climax is not solely about the action; it is about the emotional resonance of the characters' choices. As the dust settles and the climax reaches its peak, readers should feel a profound connection to the characters and their journeys. This moment will not only define the outcome of the plot but also shape the trajectory of the romance, setting the stage for the resolution that follows.

The climax is a critical element in the overall structure of an action & adventure romance story. It is where the narrative's threads converge, and the characters face their ultimate tests. By ensuring that the climax is both thrilling and emotionally charged, authors can create a memorable and impactful experience for their readers, leaving them eager to see how the story unfolds.

9

———

BUILDING TENSION

External Conflict

External conflict is a driving force in an action & adventure romance novels, propelling the narrative and engaging readers. It encompasses the tangible challenges characters face, often manifesting in high-stakes situations that demand decisive action. Understanding the various facets of external conflict is a major part of writing a good romance.

At the heart of external conflict is physical danger. Characters frequently find themselves in life-threatening scenarios that elevate the stakes and create urgency. For example, a protagonist escaping a collapsing building during an earthquake must act quickly, testing their resolve and instincts. Whether battling mercenaries on a remote island or engaging in a high-speed chase through city streets, physical danger compels characters to confront their fears and push their limits.

Incorporating time constraints can significantly amplify tension. The ticking clock serves as a reminder that characters must act swiftly to achieve their goals. A hero racing against time to defuse a bomb adds suspense, keeping readers on edge. The urgency of completing a mission before a deadline heightens stakes and forces characters to make split-second decisions, often leading to unexpected consequences that drive the narrative forward.

Utilizing the setting as an antagonist adds depth to the conflict. Environments can present formidable challenges that characters must navigate. Imagine a treacherous jungle filled with venomous snakes and unpredictable weather, where protagonists rely on survival skills to overcome obstacles. These challenges test characters' abilities and enhance overall tension, immersing readers in a dangerous world.

A formidable antagonist often serves as the catalyst for external conflict, creating direct challenges for the protagonists. The antagonist's actions can introduce complications that force characters into confrontations, testing their strengths. For instance, a cunning villain may sabotage the protagonists' efforts, leading to unexpected twists that keep readers guessing. The dynamic between protagonists and antagonists creates tension that drives the plot, compelling characters to confront their adversaries.

Introducing unexpected twists or complications maintains narrative dynamism. Surprises can range from betrayal by a trusted ally to unforeseen circumstances that alter the story's course. For example, a loyal friend revealing ulterior motives can complicate the protagonists' journey. Such complications heighten stakes and deepen character development, forcing protagonists to reevaluate their relationships and choices.

External conflict enriches action & adventure romance narratives. By weaving together physical danger, time pressure, environmental challenges, antagonist actions, and plot complications, writers create a tapestry of tension that captivates readers. This interplay of challenges propels the narrative forward and fosters character growth, making the journey as compelling as the destination.

Internal Conflict

Internal conflict is a vital component of storytelling, adding depth to characters and fostering emotional engagement. While external conflicts drive action, internal struggles resonate with readers on a personal level. By exploring your characters' inner lives, you can craft a rich narrative that captivates and holds the audience's attention.

At the core of internal conflict are personal struggles such as fears, insecurities, or moral dilemmas. For instance, a character may grapple with the fear of failure, hindering decision-making during critical plot moments. Imagine a protagonist leading a team on a dangerous expedition; their self-doubt could impact the team's survival. Showcasing these vulnerabilities creates relatable characters that draw readers deeper into the story.

Romantic relationships often serve as fertile ground for internal conflict. Jealousy, miscommunication, and differing goals can create rifts that challenge bonds. Consider a love interest feeling inadequate compared to their partner's adventurous spirit; this internal struggle may lead to misunderstandings and emotional distance, adding tension to the romance. Weaving these obstacles into the narrative enhances character development and heightens emotional stakes, making eventual resolutions more satisfying.

Characters may also face emotional barriers rooted in past traumas that hinder their ability to connect. For example, a character who has experienced loss may struggle with vulnerability, fearing that opening up will lead to further heartache. Exploring these barriers creates a nuanced portrayal, allowing readers to witness characters' journeys toward healing and connection. This depth enriches the narrative and fosters understanding of characters' motivations.

Character flaws are essential for creating relatable and complex individuals. Whether impulsive or overly cautious, these flaws can lead to internal conflicts that drive character growth. For instance, a character's excessive caution may cause them to miss critical opportunities for love or adventure. Highlighting these flaws creates a dynamic character arc that resonates with readers, showcasing the transformative power of facing inner demons.

Incorporating elements from a character's past adds emotional depth to their internal conflict. A character who has survived trauma may react differently to stressors than one with a stable upbringing. For example, if a protagonist has witnessed a loved one's betrayal, they may struggle with trust issues in their romantic relationship, leading to tension. Exploring how past experiences shape reactions to present challenges creates a rich tapestry of emotional complexity.

Internal conflict is a powerful tool for character development and emotional engagement in an action & adventure romance. By delving into personal struggles, relationship obstacles, emotional barriers, character flaws, and past trauma, you can create characters that resonate deeply with readers. This exploration of internal conflict adds depth to your narrative and enriches the reader's experience, making your story a captivating journey of growth and connection.

Scene Construction

Effective scene construction is the backbone of building tension in an action & adventure romance novel. Each scene acts as a vital piece of the narrative puzzle, contributing to the plot, character development, and emotional engagement. To captivate readers, it is essential to craft scenes that are purposeful, structured, and dynamic.

Every scene should serve a clear purpose, advancing the plot, developing characters, or enhancing overall tension. For instance, a scene where the protagonist narrowly escapes an avalanche propels the action forward and reveals their resourcefulness. This incident can set up future conflicts, such as confronting fears of nature or dealing with the consequences of choices made. Ensuring each scene is purposeful creates a cohesive narrative that resonates with readers.

A well-structured scene includes a clear goal, rising action, climax, and resolution. This structure maintains a dynamic flow that keeps readers invested. Consider a scene where the protagonist and their love interest are trapped in a crumbling cave. Their goal may be to find a way out before it collapses. As they work together, rising action builds tension—each moment of uncertainty amplifies the stakes. The climax occurs when they face a critical decision: split up to search for an exit or stay together and risk being trapped? The resolution provides relief, perhaps with one character making a sacrifice that deepens their bond. This structured approach ensures readers experience a roller-coaster of emotions.

Establishing clear goals for characters in each scene drives action and creates focus. Whether racing against time to defuse a bomb or having a heartfelt conversation, clarity enhances tension. In a scene where the protagonist must retrieve a stolen artifact before a rival, the urgency of the goal creates palpable tension, making every decision significant.

Gradually escalating conflicts within the scene build anticipation. Introduce complications or obstacles that elevate stakes. In a high-octane chase, if the protagonist's vehicle runs out of gas just as they near safety, this unexpected twist heightens tension and forces quick thinking. Each layer of conflict deepens the reader's investment in the outcome.

Each scene should peak in tension, where characters confront their greatest challenges. This moment often leads to significant character development or plot revelations. For instance, during a climactic confrontation with the antagonist, the protagonist may finally face their deepest fears, revealing their true strength. This pivotal moment drives the plot forward and allows for emotional growth, making it a powerful turning point.

A satisfying resolution ties up loose ends while leaving room for further development. This can provide a moment of relief or reflection for characters, allowing readers to process the emotional journey. After a harrowing escape, a scene might conclude with the protagonists sharing a quiet moment, reflecting on their experiences and deepening their connection. This resolution closes immediate conflict while setting the stage for future challenges.

Incorporating these elements of effective scene construction creates a rich tapestry of tension that captivates readers and drives character growth throughout the narrative. By ensuring each scene is purposeful, structured, and dynamic, you can maintain excitement and emotional engagement in your action & adventure romance novel.

10

———

MASTERING DIALOGUE TECHNIQUES

Character Voice

in an action & adventure romance, dialogue is a powerful tool that brings characters to life, making their voices resonate with readers. A distinct character voice is essential for differentiation and allows characters to stand out in the narrative. Each character should have a unique way of speaking that reflects their background, personality, and emotional state, creating a rich tapestry of interactions that enhances the story.

Distinct speaking patterns vividly illustrate a character's essence. For example, a confident hero may use short, decisive statements, reflecting their self-assured nature. Faced with a challenge, they might declare, "We need to act now," showcasing their readiness to take charge. In contrast, a hesitant character may pepper their speech with qualifiers, saying, "Do you think we should...?" This contrast highlights their differences and invites readers to engage with their unique perspectives.

Dialogue serves as an intimate window into a character's psyche, allowing readers to glean insights into their motivations and feelings. A character's emotional state can dramatically influence their communication style. During moments of high tension, a character experiencing anxiety might speak in fragmented sentences, revealing their inner turmoil: "I can't believe this is happening. What do we do?" Such dialogue captures the urgency of the moment and draws readers deeper into the character's experience.

A character's background profoundly shapes their communication style. Factors such as education, upbringing, and life experiences inform their vocabulary and speech patterns. A character raised in a formal environment may articulate their thoughts with sophistication, using phrases like "I must respectfully disagree." Conversely, a character from a casual background might say, "I don't think that's right." This contrast enriches dialogue and provides context for the characters' interactions and relationships.

Emotional state plays a pivotal role in how characters express themselves. Stressed or excited characters often speak more quickly, their words tumbling out in a rush. During a thrilling chase scene, for instance, a character might exclaim, "We have to go, now!" The urgency of their speech mirrors the intensity of the moment, heightening the reader's adrenaline. In contrast, calm characters may adopt a more measured pace, allowing their dialogue to flow smoothly. This variation in pacing reflects the characters' emotional landscapes and engages readers on a deeper level.

By making distinct character voices, authors create a dynamic interplay of dialogue that captivates readers. Each character's unique way of speaking enriches the narrative, allowing for a more immersive reading experience. As characters navigate their thrilling adventures and romantic entanglements, their voices become vital in conveying their journeys, emotions, and relationships, ultimately enhancing the story's impact.

Emotional Impact

Creating emotional impact through dialogue is one of the most powerful tools a writer can wield. It is in the spaces between words—where hesitation, longing, and vulnerability reside—that readers can truly connect with characters. Establishing a deep connection between characters is essential, allowing readers to experience their feelings intimately. A deep point of view can enhance this connection, immersing readers in the characters' emotional landscapes. When crafted with intimacy in mind, dialogue transcends mere conversation and transforms into a conduit for emotional resonance.

Emotional truth is paramount in dialogue. Characters must express genuine feelings, steering clear of clichés that can alienate readers. For instance, if a character grapples with the loss of a loved one, their dialogue should reflect the rawness of that grief—perhaps through fragmented sentences or a reluctance to speak at all. When a character says, "I just don't know how to breathe without them," it encapsulates the weight of their sorrow, drawing readers into their pain. Such expressions resonate deeply, echoing the experiences of readers who may have faced similar losses.

Relatable feelings in dialogue foster empathy. When characters articulate their struggles or joys in relatable ways, it deepens readers' investment in their journeys. Consider a scene where a character confesses their fear of failure before an important event: "What if I mess this up? What if I'm not good enough?" This vulnerability invites readers to reflect on their own fears, creating a bond that transcends the page. By expressing common emotional experiences, writers can create characters that feel like friends, whose triumphs and failures matter.

Natural reactions in dialogue are crucial for authenticity. Characters should respond to events and conversations in ways that reflect real-life reactions. For instance, if a character receives shocking news, their initial response might be silence, followed by a stammered, "What? No, that can't be true." This realistic portrayal of shock enhances believability, allowing readers to feel the weight of the moment alongside the character.

The emotional journey of the reader is shaped by how well dialogue conveys the characters' experiences. Memorable moments of connection or conflict can leave a lasting impact, ensuring that readers remain invested in the story. A poignant exchange between characters, where one reveals a long-held secret, can shift their relationship dynamics and resonate with readers long after the page is turned. For example, when a character finally admits, "I've loved you all along, but I was too scared to say it," the raw honesty can evoke tears, laughter, or a bittersweet ache, depending on the context.

The emotional impact of dialogue is critical in Writing compelling narratives. By establishing deep connections, ensuring emotional truth, fostering relatability, and maintaining authenticity in reactions, writers can create dialogue that resonates powerfully with readers. This emotional engagement enhances the reading experience and solidifies the bond between characters and their audience, making the story unforgettable.

Dialogue Functions

Dialogue serves multiple essential functions in storytelling, contributing to a compelling narrative. in an action & adventure romance, where stakes are high and emotions run deep, effective dialogue can propel the plot, reveal character depth, build relationships, and create tension. Understanding these functions enhances writing and engages readers on a profound level.

Advancing the plot is one of dialogue's primary roles. Conversations convey crucial information that drives the action forward, maintaining the story's momentum. For instance, imagine the protagonist, a daring treasure hunter named Maya, racing against time to uncover a lost artifact before a rival can seize it. During a tense exchange with her mentor, she learns that the artifact is hidden in a treacherous jungle, guarded by ancient traps. This revelation propels Maya into the next phase of her adventure and raises the stakes, drawing readers into her quest.

In a romantic subplot, Maya's love interest, a brooding archaeologist named Ethan, reveals a secret about his past that complicates their relationship. He might say, "I never wanted to drag you into this. My family has a history with that artifact, and it's dangerous." This line provides essential backstory while heightening the tension between them, creating immediate conflict that readers will want to see resolved.

Dialogue also serves as a window into the characters' inner worlds, allowing readers to grasp their motivations, fears, and desires. For example, if Maya speaks confidently with assertive statements like, "We have to go now," it showcases her determination. In contrast, if she hesitates and says, "I think we should maybe reconsider," it reveals her internal struggle, making her more relatable.

In a moment of vulnerability, Ethan might express his reluctance to trust by saying, "Every time I let someone in, they end up getting hurt." This statement reveals his emotional scars and deepens the reader's understanding of his character. Weaving these layers into dialogue creates a richer, more nuanced portrayal that resonates with readers.

Building relationships is another crucial function of dialogue. It can showcase emotional bonds or highlight conflicts that create tension. During a heated argument, Maya might snap, "You don't get to decide what's best for me!" This line reflects her independence while illustrating the friction in her relationship with Ethan, who may be trying to protect her. Such exchanges create a push-and-pull dynamic that keeps readers invested in the characters' journeys.

Conversely, lighter moments can also contribute to relationship-building. Imagine a scene where Maya and Ethan share a laugh over a near-miss with a booby trap. Their banter might include playful teasing, such as Maya quipping, "Next time, I'll let you take the lead," followed by Ethan's retort, "As long as you promise to keep the snacks coming." This lighthearted exchange showcases their chemistry and deepens their connection, making their eventual romantic moments more impactful.

Finally, dialogue can create tension, which is essential in an action & adventure romance. When characters have opposing objectives, their conversations can become charged with conflict. For example, if Maya insists on pursuing the artifact despite the danger, and Ethan argues against it, their dialogue could escalate:

Maya: "I can't just walk away from this. It's my only chance to prove myself!"

Ethan: "And what if you don't come back? Is that worth the risk?"

This exchange heightens the stakes, drawing readers into the emotional struggle between the characters. The tension created through dialogue keeps readers on the edge of their seats, eager to find out how the conflict will resolve.

The functions of dialogue in an action & adventure romance are multifaceted and integral to storytelling. By mastering dialogue that advances the plot, reveals character depth, builds relationships, and creates tension, you can craft a narrative that captivates readers and keeps them invested in your characters' journeys. Remember that every line of dialogue is an opportunity to deepen your story and connect with your audience.

11

REVISING YOUR WORK: AVOIDING COMMON PITFALLS

Revision Process: Drafting and Feedback

The revision process is a crucial stage in Writing a best-selling action & adventure romance novel. Writers must approach their drafts with an open mind, recognizing that the initial version is merely a stepping stone toward a polished manuscript. No first draft is perfect; it serves as the foundation for the final structure.

Multiple drafts allow writers to explore various angles, deepen characterizations, and refine plot intricacies. Each iteration reveals new layers within the narrative. For instance, a character initially defined by their role in the action may, through revisions, emerge with a rich backstory that adds emotional depth and complexity to the plot.

Feedback from beta readers is invaluable in this process. These readers, ideally representing your target audience, provide fresh perspectives that can illuminate weaknesses in plot, pacing, or character development. Their insights can reveal how well the story resonates with readers and highlight areas needing improvement. For example, a beta reader might point out that a key romantic moment lacks tension or that an action sequence feels rushed.

Incorporating this feedback is essential for refining themes and enhancing emotional impact. When receiving constructive criticism, approach it with a growth mindset. Instead of feeling defensive, view it as an opportunity to elevate your work. If a reader suggests that a subplot feels disconnected from the main storyline, this is your chance to weave it back into the narrative, enriching the overall experience.

Professional editing is also a cornerstone of the revision process. While beta readers provide valuable insights, a professional editor brings expertise in polishing prose, ensuring clarity, and maintaining pacing. Their keen eye can catch inconsistencies, awkward phrasing, or areas where the narrative may lag. For instance, an editor might suggest tightening a dialogue exchange to enhance its emotional weight or restructuring a chapter to improve the flow of action and romance.

Ultimately, the revision process is about transformation. It involves taking the rough diamond of a first draft and chiseling away the excess to reveal its brilliance. By engaging deeply with your manuscript through multiple drafts, actively seeking feedback, and embracing professional editing, you will create a narrative that captivates readers and resonates emotionally. This commitment to revision will set your action & adventure romance novel apart in a competitive market, ensuring it has the depth, excitement, and emotional resonance necessary for success.

Common Plot Issues: Avoiding Predictability

One significant pitfall in writing is delivering predictable storylines that fail to engage readers. Predictability often arises from weak conflicts or clichéd resolutions, creating a narrative that lacks the excitement necessary to keep an audience invested. To craft a compelling action & adventure romance, writers must actively avoid these traps by embracing originality and creativity in their plots.

Introducing unexpected twists can breathe new life into a narrative. For instance, imagine a hero embarking on a quest to rescue a kidnapped love interest. Instead of a straightforward rescue mission leading to a happy ending, the writer might reveal that the love interest has been working with the captors, driven by a desire for revenge against the hero. This twist surprises readers and deepens the emotional stakes, forcing both characters to confront their motivations and the complexities of their relationship.

Character decisions should be rooted in established motivations that feel authentic. For example, if a character is fiercely independent, it would be predictable for them to accept help without hesitation. A more engaging narrative would show them grappling with their desire for autonomy while recognizing the necessity of collaboration to overcome obstacles. This internal conflict adds layers to the plot, creating tension that keeps readers on the edge of their seats.

Another critical aspect to consider is the potential for plot holes—gaps in logic or unresolved threads that can disrupt the reader's immersion. If a character suddenly acquires a skill essential to the plot without prior indication, it can feel jarring. Thorough planning and outlining are essential strategies to identify these issues early. Writers should ensure that every development in the plot is grounded in the characters' established traits and experiences, maintaining continuity and believability.

Writers should also challenge themselves to place characters in situations where they must confront their deepest fears or make difficult choices. This can elevate tension and intrigue, as readers become invested not only in the plot's outcome but also in the characters' emotional journeys. For example, a protagonist might face a moral dilemma that forces them to choose between saving their love interest or preventing a greater disaster. This choice should stem from their personal growth, ensuring that the stakes feel high and the resolution impactful.

Ultimately, avoiding predictability in writing requires a commitment to originality, character depth, and logical coherence. By striving for unexpected twists, grounding character actions in authentic motivations, and eliminating plot holes through careful planning, writers can create narratives that captivate and resonate with readers. In the realm of action & adventure romance, where emotional stakes run high and excitement is paramount, these strategies will leave a lasting impression.

Character Problems: Ensuring Growth

Character development is a cornerstone of any engaging action & adventure romance novel. When readers invest in characters, they forge emotional connections with their journeys, triumphs, and failures. However, many writers falter in this area, resulting in flat personalities and forced romances that detract from the overall narrative. To create compelling characters, it is essential to ensure they grow and evolve throughout the story.

Characters must embody relatable flaws and strengths, allowing readers to see themselves in them. For instance, a protagonist grappling with self-doubt while exhibiting courage can resonate deeply. This blend of vulnerability and strength not only makes the character relatable but also sets the stage for meaningful growth.

Authentic growth is paramount. Characters should not remain static; they must evolve by confronting both internal and external conflicts that challenge their beliefs and motivations. Consider a character who begins as a reckless adventurer, driven solely by the thrill of danger. As the narrative unfolds, they may encounter a love interest who compels them to confront their fear of vulnerability. This encounter can lead to a transformation, where the character learns to balance their adventurous spirit with emotional openness, creating a richer, more nuanced personality.

It is crucial that character actions and decisions are justified within the narrative. Poorly motivated characters can lead to reader disengagement, making it essential for writers to ensure that every choice stems from established motivations. If a character suddenly betrays a close ally without a clear reason, it can feel forced. Instead, their decisions should reflect their growth, struggles, and the stakes involved. When faced with a dilemma that tests their moral compass, the resolution should feel earned and believable.

Furthermore, writers should focus on Writing character arcs that reflect genuine transformation. This means allowing characters to face challenges that force them to confront their flaws and adapt. For example, a character who starts as a lone wolf may learn the value of teamwork when confronted by a formidable antagonist. This evolution enhances the character's depth and enriches the plot, as their newfound perspective influences key decisions and outcomes.

Symbolizing character growth is a great part of writing in this genre. By creating relatable characters with authentic flaws and strengths, justifying their actions, and allowing them to evolve through meaningful experiences, writers can create a narrative that resonates with readers emotionally. This depth enhances individual character journeys and elevates the overall story, making it a memorable and immersive experience for the audience.

12

EFFECTIVE PUBLISHING AND MARKETING STRATEGIES

Traditional Publishing

Traditional publishing has long been considered the gold standard for aspiring authors. This route typically involves submitting query letters to literary agents and publishers, a process that can be daunting but is essential for those seeking representation for their action & adventure romance novels.

The first step in this journey is conducting thorough research on agents and publishers who specialize in the action & adventure romance genre. Understanding the nuances of this genre is crucial, as it helps authors identify which agents are likely to be interested in their work. Websites like QueryTracker and Manuscript Wish List are invaluable resources for locating agents actively seeking submissions in this niche. The goal is to find someone who appreciates the genre and resonates with your unique voice and story.

Once potential agents have been identified, the next step is to carefully review their submission guidelines. Each agent or publisher may have specific requirements regarding the format of the query letter, sample chapters, and the type of work they are seeking. Adhering to these guidelines is critical; a well-crafted query that follows the specified instructions can significantly enhance your chances of acceptance. For example, if an agent requests a one-page synopsis, submitting a two-page version could lead to an automatic rejection.

Understanding the market is another vital aspect of traditional publishing. Authors must create a marketable concept that aligns with genre expectations and appeals to their target audience. This involves being aware of current trends in an action & adventure romance and recognizing successful titles and their key elements. Novels like "The Night Circus" by Erin Morgenstern and "Outlander" by Diana Gabaldon effectively blend elements of romance and adventure, setting a benchmark for aspiring authors.

The benefits of traditional publishing are numerous. Authors gain access to established distribution channels, enhancing the reach of their books. Additionally, professional editing services and marketing support from the publisher can elevate the quality and visibility of the work. A well-edited manuscript can significantly impact reader engagement and critical reception, reflecting a level of professionalism that self-published works may sometimes lack.

However, traditional publishing also has drawbacks. The process from acceptance to publication can take a year or more, and authors may experience less creative control over their work, as publishers typically have the final say on aspects such as cover design and marketing strategies. Moreover, the royalty rates offered by traditional publishers tend to be lower compared to self-publishing, where authors retain a larger portion of their sales.

Traditional publishing offers a structured path for authors of action & adventure romance novels, complete with industry support and established distribution channels. However, it requires careful research, adherence to submission guide-lines, and a strong understanding of market dynamics. For those willing to navigate this complex landscape, the rewards can be substantial, paving the way for a successful writing career.

Self-Publishing

Self-publishing has become a powerful avenue for authors, especially in the action & adventure romance genre, who seek creative freedom and a direct connection with their audience. This path allows writers to maintain complete control over their work, from content to cover design, making autonomy an essential aspect of their artistic expression.

One of the most appealing features of self-publishing is the ability to infuse a personal touch into every aspect of the book. Authors can select cover designs that resonate with their vision, choose formatting that suits their narrative style, and craft marketing messages that reflect their unique voice. This level of control can lead to a more authentic representation of the author's intent, which is particularly important in a genre that thrives on emotional depth and thrilling escapades.

However, with great freedom comes great responsibility. Quality control is paramount in self-publishing. Authors must ensure that their work meets high standards of professionalism to compete in a crowded marketplace. Hiring professional editors is crucial; a skilled editor can refine the manuscript, enhancing clarity and coherence while ensuring that the pacing of action and romance is finely tuned. Similarly, investing in a professional cover designer can significantly elevate the book's visual appeal, as a captivating cover can be the difference between a potential reader clicking "buy" or scrolling past.

Once the book is polished and ready for release, developing a robust marketing plan becomes essential. Unlike traditional publishing, where marketing support is often provided by the publisher, self-published authors must actively promote their work. This includes leveraging various channels such as social media platforms, author websites, and newsletters to reach potential readers. A well-crafted author website can serve as a central hub for branding, showcasing not only the book but also the author's journey, insights, and future projects.

Social media engagement is another critical component of a successful marketing strategy. Authors should create interactive content to foster a sense of community among readers. Hosting Q&A sessions, running giveaways, and conducting polls can create a dynamic relationship with the audience, encouraging them to invest in the author's journey and upcoming works. This engagement builds loyalty and generates buzz around the book's release.

A comprehensive promotion plan should also include a launch strategy that outlines specific actions to maximize visibility. This could involve pre-release activities, such as garnering reviews from beta readers and influencers, and coordinating blog tours that introduce the book to new audiences. Collaborating with other authors for cross-promotion can further expand reach, allowing each author to tap into the established readership of their peers.

Finally, understanding distribution is critical for self-published authors. Platforms like Amazon KDP and IngramSpark offer vast opportunities for distribution, but each has its nuances. Authors must familiarize themselves with these platforms to maximize their book's reach and sales potential. Additionally, considering direct sales through personal websites can create a more intimate purchasing experience for readers, allowing authors to retain a larger percentage of the profits.

Self-publishing represents a landscape of opportunity and challenge for authors in the action & adventure romance genre. By embracing quality control, developing a strategic marketing plan, and understanding distribution channels, authors can carve out a successful path in the ever-evolving publishing world. The journey may be demanding, but the rewards of creative freedom and direct reader engagement make it a fulfilling endeavor for those willing to invest the time and effort.

Marketing Strategies

in an action & adventure romance, an author's journey extends far beyond completing a manuscript. To transform a well-crafted story into a bestseller, effective marketing strategies are essential. A robust marketing plan is crucial not only for reaching potential readers but also for establishing a lasting author brand. Here, we explore key components of successful marketing strategies tailored for action & adventure romance authors.

Platform Building

The cornerstone of any successful marketing strategy is platform building. An author website serves as the central hub for branding, showcasing published works, insights into the writing process, character backstories, and upcoming projects. A well-designed website creates a professional image that resonates with readers.

In addition to a website, cultivating a strong social media presence is vital. Platforms such as Instagram, TikTok, and Facebook enable authors to connect directly with their audience. Sharing snippets of writing, behind-the-scenes glimpses, and personal anecdotes fosters intimacy and community among readers. Engaging content—such as polls, questions, and interactive stories—keeps followers invested and encourages them to spread the word about your books.

Moreover, building a newsletter list is an invaluable strategy. Regular updates about new releases, exclusive content, and personal reflections keep your audience engaged and eager for your next book. Offering a free short story or a sneak peek of your upcoming release in exchange for email sign-ups can effectively grow your list.

Engaging with Readers

Creating a loyal reader base goes beyond mere promotion; it requires genuine engagement. Interactive content plays a pivotal role in this process. Hosting Q&A sessions on social media or through your website invites readers to ask questions about your writing, characters, and storylines, fostering a deeper connection.

Giveaways can generate excitement and encourage sharing among readers. Consider offering signed copies of your book, themed merchandise, or exclusive content to entice participation. Polls and surveys provide valuable insights into reader preferences, allowing you to tailor future works to meet their desires.

Building a community around your writing enhances reader loyalty and generates invaluable word-of-mouth promotion in the crowded book market.

Comprehensive Promotion Plan

A comprehensive promotion plan is essential for maximizing visibility and sales. Start by developing a launch strategy that includes a timeline for pre-release teasers, cover reveals, and countdowns to build anticipation. Consider utilizing targeted advertisements on social media to reach specific demographics interested in an action & adventure romance.

Acquiring reviews is another critical component. Reach out to book bloggers, reviewers, and influencers in the genre to request honest feedback. Positive reviews significantly influence purchasing decisions, and a solid review base enhances your book's credibility.

Coordinating blog tours can also increase visibility. Partnering with fellow authors or bloggers to feature your book on their platforms introduces your work to new audiences. This cross-promotion can be mutually beneficial, expanding reach for all parties involved.

Adapting to Market Trends

The publishing landscape is ever-evolving, and successful authors must stay attuned to market trends. Understanding which themes, settings, and character archetypes resonate with readers can inform your writing and marketing strategies. For instance, if there is a rising interest in diverse characters or settings, consider integrating those elements into your stories to align with reader preferences.

Regularly reviewing sales data, reader feedback, and industry news provides insights into shifting trends. Adapting your marketing strategies ensures that you remain relevant and can capitalize on emerging opportunities in the action & adventure romance genre.

An author's journey in the action & adventure romance genre encompasses more than Writing a compelling narrative. Building a strong platform, engaging with readers, implementing a comprehensive promotion plan, and adapting to market trends are essential for long-term success. By investing time and effort into these marketing strategies, authors can enhance their visibility and cultivate a loyal readership that eagerly anticipates their next adventure.